George Tscherny:

Where would the button be without the button hole?

Unsung heroes of anonymous design

RIT CARY
GRAPHIC ARTS
PRESS

George Tscherny:
Where would the button be
without the button hole?
Unsung heroes of anonymous design

RIT Graphic Arts Press
90 Lomb Memorial Drive
Rochester, New York 14623-5604
http://carypress.rit.edu

Printed in the United States

ISBN 978-1933360-35-5

Design & photography: George Tscherny; George Tscherny, Inc.
Production assistant: Ryan Durinick; George Tscherny, Inc.

Production/RIT: Marnie Soom; Amelia Hugill-Fontanel; Molly Cort

Printing: Monroe Litho
Paper: Cover: 130 lb. McCoy Silk Text: 100 lb. McCoy Silk
Typefaces: Futura; Gill Sans; Gill Sans Bold; Gill Sans Extra Bold

"For the historian there are no banal things."

Siegfried Gideon
Mechanization Takes Command
Oxford University Press, 1948

Foreword

This book is about designs born of necessity; often spontaneously, always pragmatically. It is also about the particular sensibility of George Tscherny and his ability to find beauty or art in the most ordinary things and more importantly to communicate this appreciation to others. As his daughter, I have long witnessed George's infectious enthusiasm for what could be called "anonymous," "ad hoc," or "vernacular" design, for objects that have an aesthetic appeal in spite of themselves, for creations that are both ingenious and ingenuous.

Growing up, I was surrounded not only by classics of modern design that one might expect in the home of a graphic designer, but also by George's various collections and "museums" – assorted curious objects, seldom encountered in that pre-eBay era, which he delighted in showing to guests who would try to guess their function. A devout but not doctrinaire modernist, George relishes "casting doubt on the inevitability of progress" as we see in his celebration of the vintage re-closeable bottle here. Now, when waste and refuse are compelling issues, descendents of these quirky bottles which George collected are making a comeback. Will the revival of the quaint Folding Lunch Box pictured here be next?

"*Maximum utility / minimum means*" is more than a modernist credo to George who, like an archaeologist, unearths the origins of the industrial aesthetic in the artlessly fashioned paper clip, safety pin and wire hanger. If these tools of metal and plastic recall the basic human urge to adapt and flourish, their graphic equivalents – abstract and universal signs or symbols such as the arrow which George follows with characteristic humor and interest – recall the equally basic human desire to communicate. The urgent scrawls of public graffiti or the handprint next to the bathroom sign, like some prehistoric cave markings, go beyond communication to unfettered personal expression, seemingly far from the discipline of typography and graphic design, but close to George's heart. The three-page spread on measuring instruments might for a moment look like a jewelry display, as these purely functional devices are undoubtedly, though unintentionally, beautiful in their rhythms, materials, and graduated forms. These are just a sampling of the many objects George has collected, and this book gives the reader a glimpse into his world. Like the question, "Where would the button be without the button hole?" It is food for thought.

Nadia Tscherny April 2008

Casting doubt on the inevitability of progress

In the early 60s, the aluminum industry announced with great fanfare the "innovation" of a new can with a pull tab lid, making the can opener superfluous.

Nothing was said of the time-proven bottles which could be opened *and* closed keeping the beverage fresh for a later helping.

These bottles came in a great variety of shapes, sizes and materials. Recycled bottles were cleaned, received a new rubber washer and were as good as new.

While the ruling taste in the 19th century demanded ornamentation and embellishment, the introduction of mass production techniques resulted in a machine aesthetic that created its own source of beauty.

With metal replacing wood for many products, inventiveness and manufacturing skill developed forms peculiar to machine mass production.

Notably ingenious was the use of bent wire, which in one continuous line produced, for example, a coat and hat hook that required no screws and tools to be installed or removed.

Maximum utility minimum means!

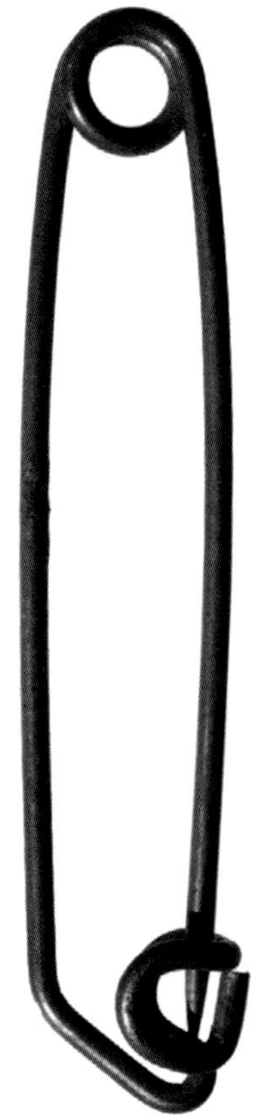

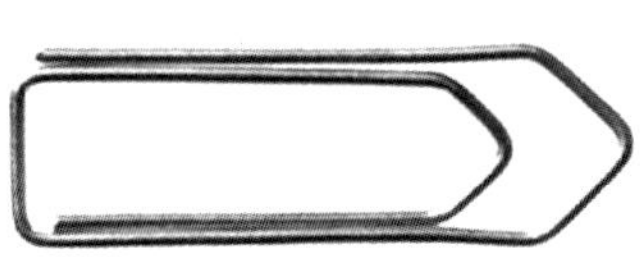

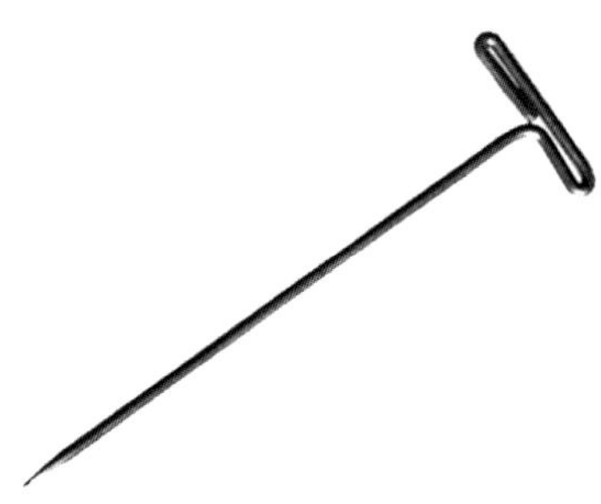

CHAMPAGNE

On the move...

Whether around the globe or just around the block, the lighter the burden, the more pleasant the trip. Traveling comfortably means less bulk as well as less weight.

Here are some examples of size reduction, past and present.

Just keep folding!

One would hardly expect this aptly named MIDGET to telescope into a full-size coat hanger.

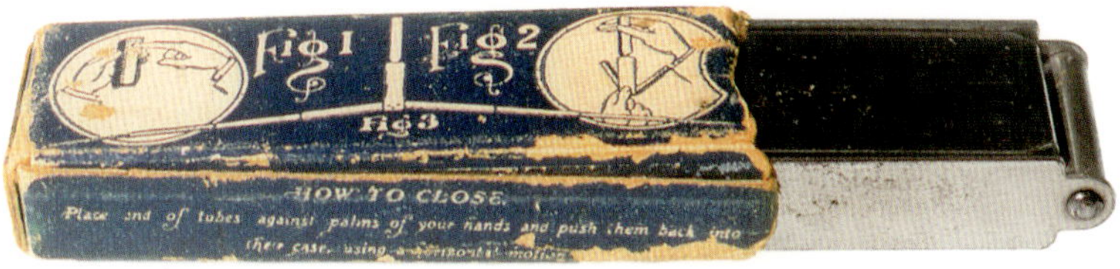

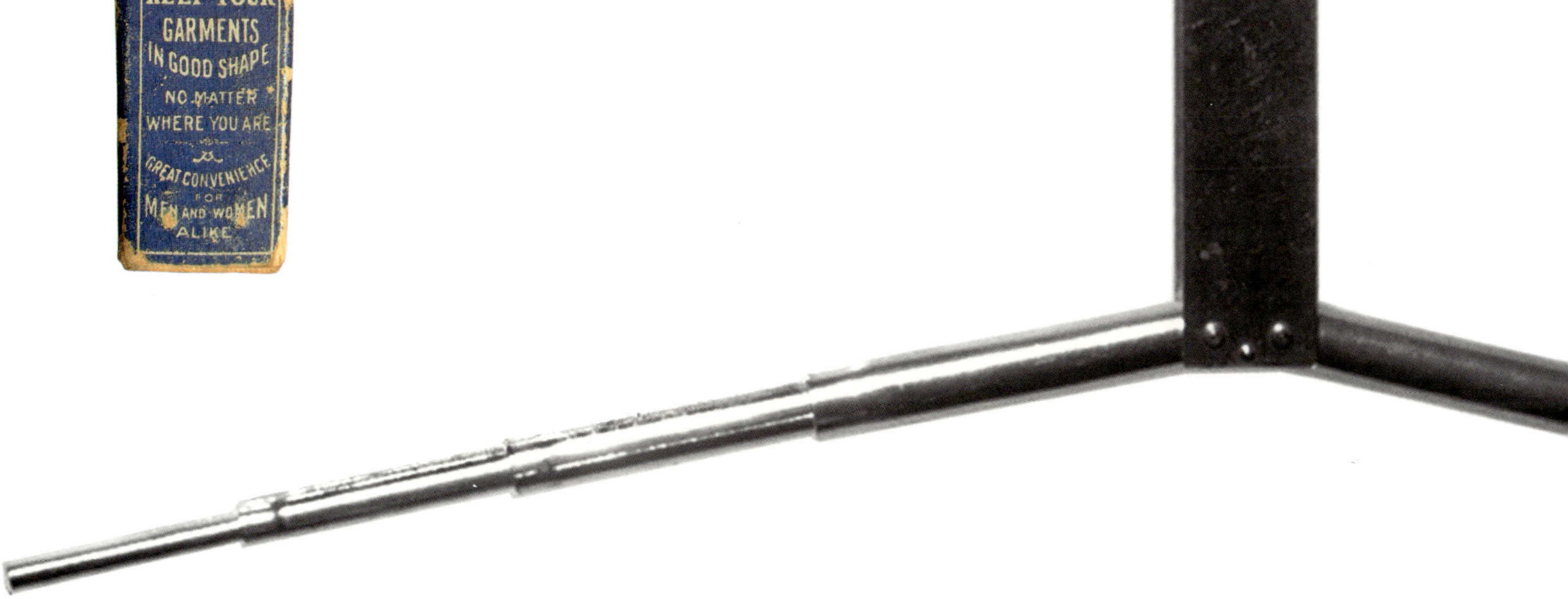

The hinged panels of this lunch box unfold when needed and collapse to a slim packet after the lunch has been eaten.

Prior to the development of the cylinder lock and the resultant small flat key, keys were very bulky. Folding them in half, like a pocket knife, reduced them to half their size making them more "pocket friendly."

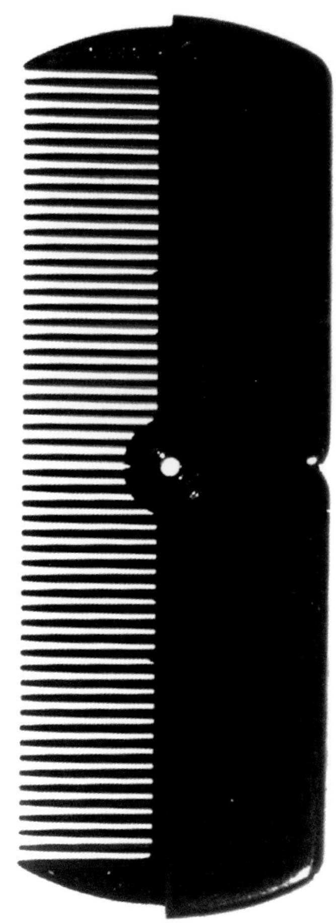

As if it had burst from a coccoon, this mysterious object reveals itself to be a pocket comb.

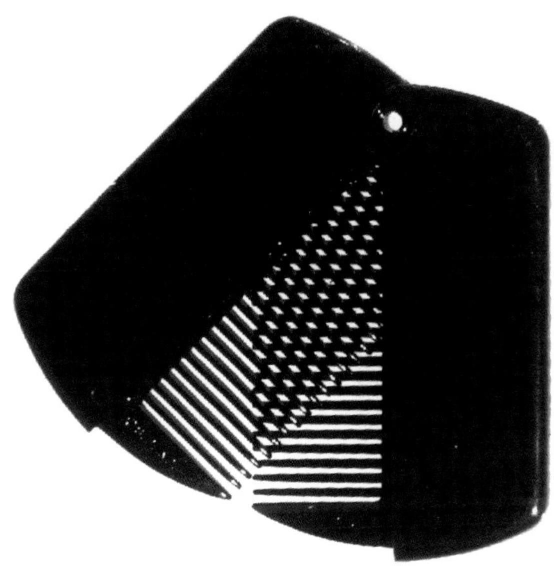

Much like origami,
this matchbook-size package unfolds
to become a disposable razor.

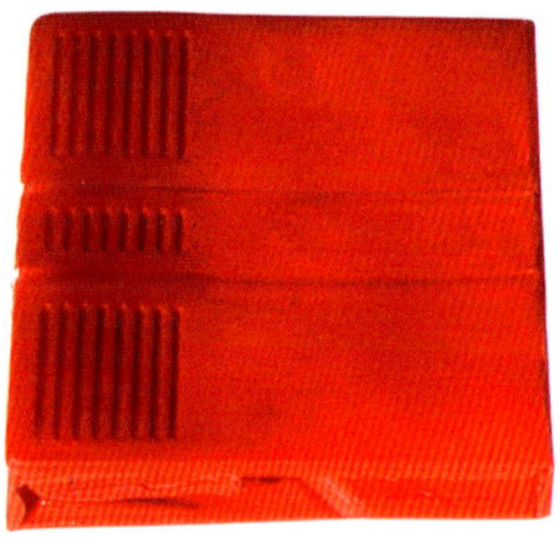

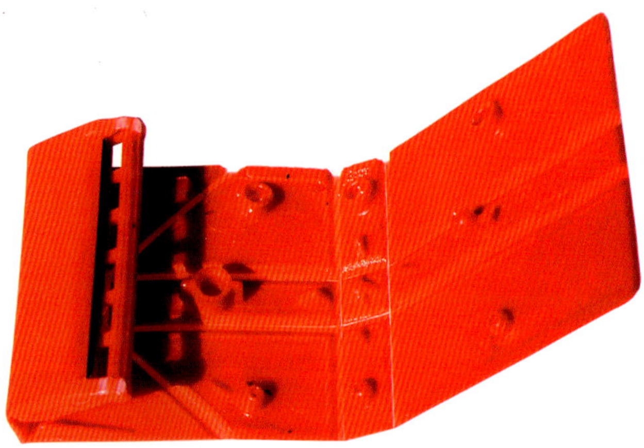

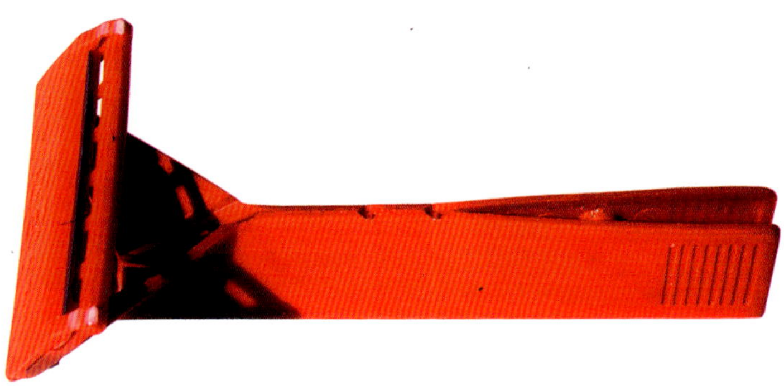

Hung from a chain
or in a pocket,
scissors are safest
in a collapsed state.

These are hats with a memory. A built-in steel wire lets the collapsed hat snap into shape.

The opera hat came first...
The sun hat, some 200 years later.

That-a-way

The arrow has replaced the finger as a directional device. It can point in two directions simultaneously, which the finger never could.

This is not what was meant by pointing "in two directions simultaneously."

Simply turning the sign will guide the pedestrian in the opposite direction.

The arrow knows no language barrier, it communicates with greater accuracy than words and does so instantly.

"I'll just be a minute."

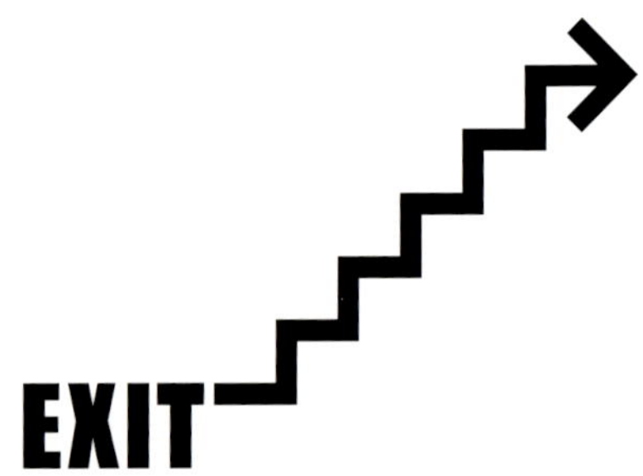

Together with add-ons one can instruct "exit upstairs," admonish "curb your dog," or receive Cupid's message of love.

LA TOUR

Voices

Public spaces readily accept confrontational messages that would not be acceptable in more conventional venues.

Extremes of love and hate can find expression there, but love is transitory as the crossed out or changed names demonstrate.

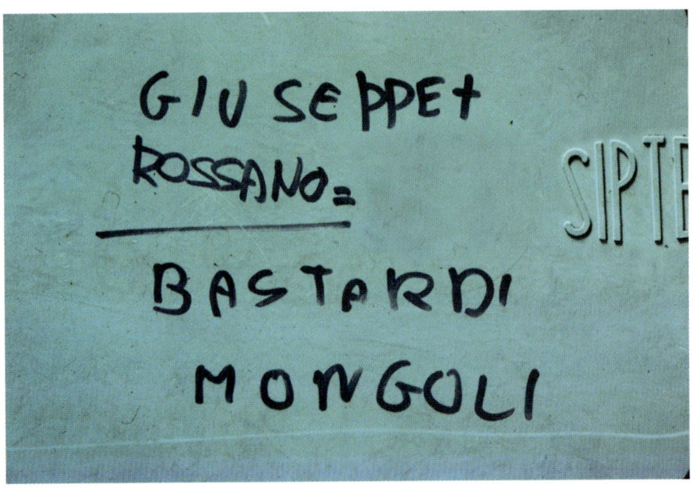

MARGIE +
NANCY
LENA
BOBBY

Measure for measure

S M L XL – size matters. The importance of standards is critical to business practices.

Defining units of weights and measures was attempted as early as the Magna Carta, but only in the 19th century was a uniform metric system established in Europe.

Efforts in the U.S. to convert to the metric system have repeatedly faltered, complicating international trade and scientific development.

For the graphic designer, the designation of page formats is a recurrent problem.

Americans, for example, specify letter size in inches, (8 1/2 × 11″). Internationally, letter size is designated by a letter and number combination (A4) derived from the metric measurement which measures (8 1/4 × 11 11/16″).

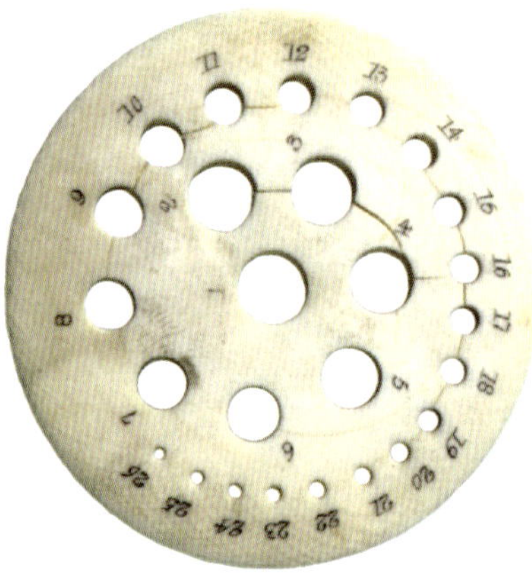

Ivory gauge for measuring (knitting) needles

Wire and sheet metal gauge

Gauge for measuring size of apples

Pocket gauge – measures fingers for ring size

Ring stick to determine ring diameter

A gauge with a full complement of ring sizes

Gauge for checking radii
of tools, dies, patterns, etc.

Sampler of brass sheet thickness

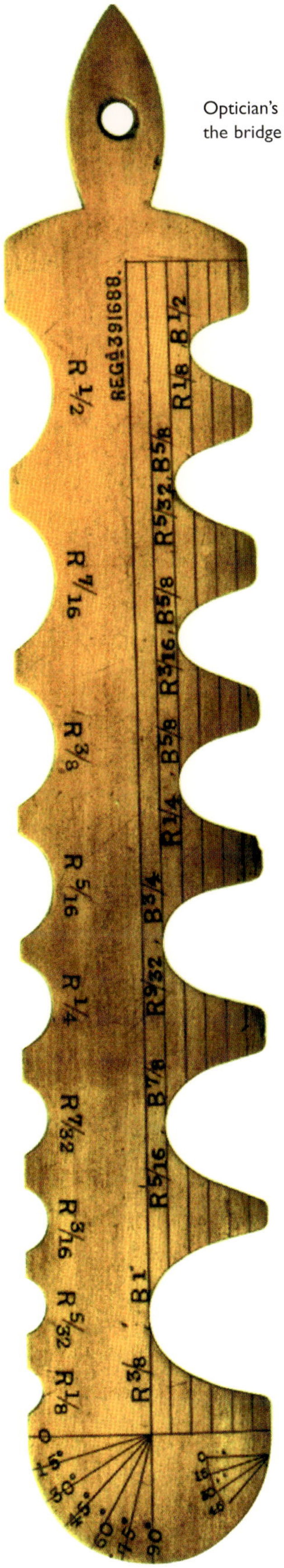

Optician's rule for measuring the bridge of the nose

What is it?

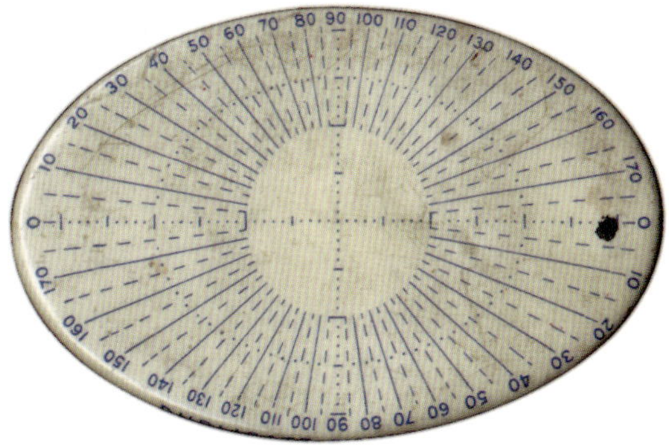

The reverse side carries this text and diagram.

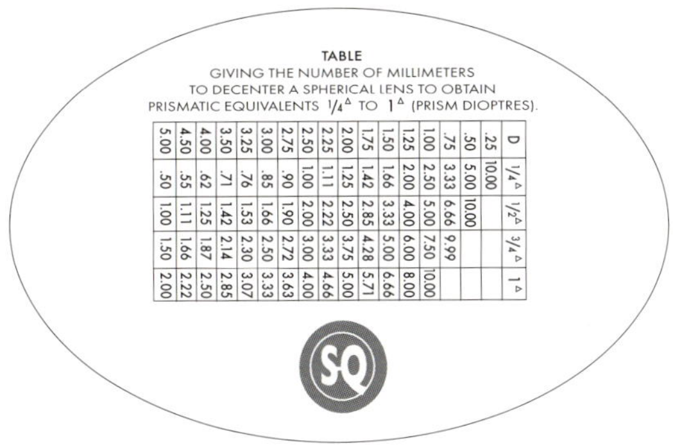

TABLE
GIVING THE NUMBER OF MILLIMETERS
TO DECENTER A SPHERICAL LENS TO OBTAIN
PRISMATIC EQUIVALENTS $1/4^{\Delta}$ TO 1^{Δ} (PRISM DIOPTRES).

D	$1/4^{\Delta}$	$1/2^{\Delta}$	$3/4^{\Delta}$	1^{Δ}
.25	10.00			
.50	5.00	10.00		
.75	3.33	6.66	9.99	
1.00	2.50	5.00	7.50	10.00
1.25	2.00	4.00	6.00	8.00
1.50	1.66	3.33	5.00	6.66
1.75	1.42	2.85	4.28	5.71
2.00	1.25	2.50	3.75	5.00
2.25	1.11	2.22	3.33	4.66
2.50	1.00	2.00	3.00	4.00
2.75	.90	1.90	2.72	3.63
3.00	.85	1.66	2.50	3.33
3.25	.76	1.53	2.30	3.07
3.50	.71	1.42	2.14	2.85
4.00	.62	1.25	1.87	2.50
4.50	.55	1.11	1.66	2.22
5.00	.50	1.00	1.50	2.00

Now you know all we know.

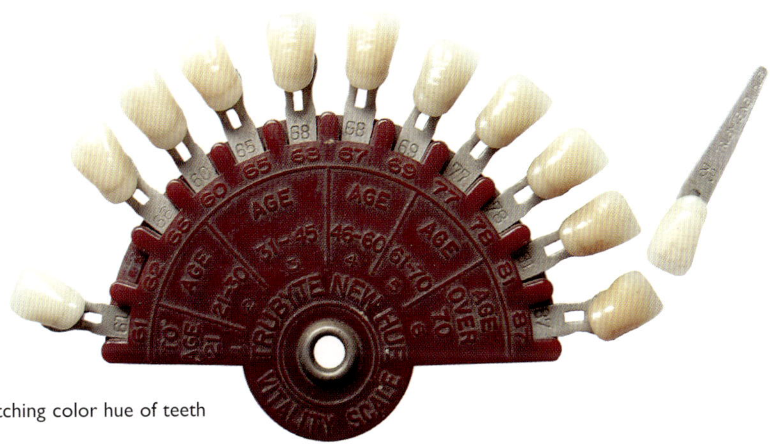

Scale for matching color hue of teeth

Gauge to determine the pitch of screw threads

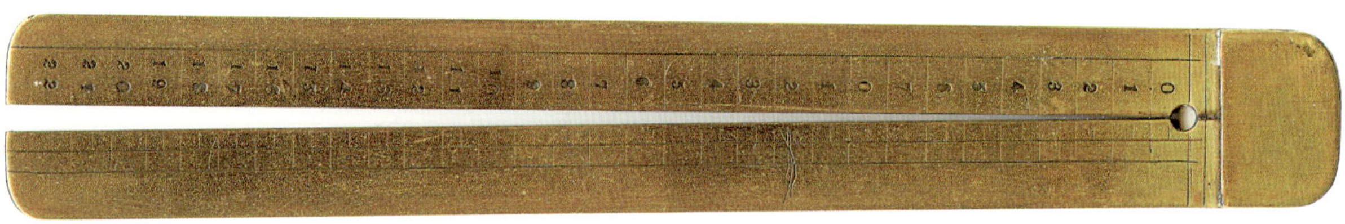

Gauge for measuring musical instrument strings

Thickness gauge (or feeler)

Gauge used in the manufacture of wax candles

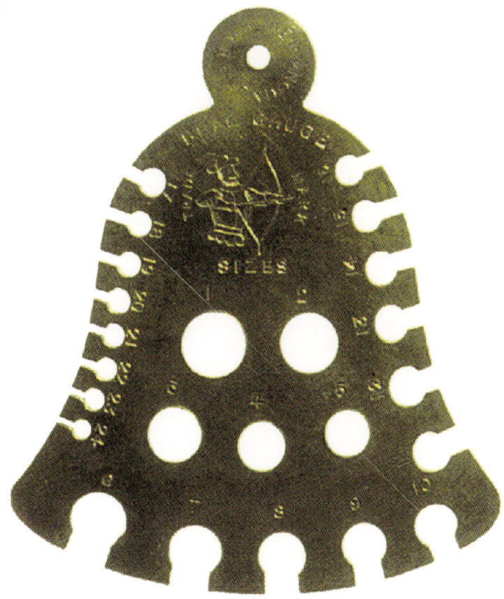

"Bell" gauge for wire and sheet metal

Center gauge for finding the number of threads per inch

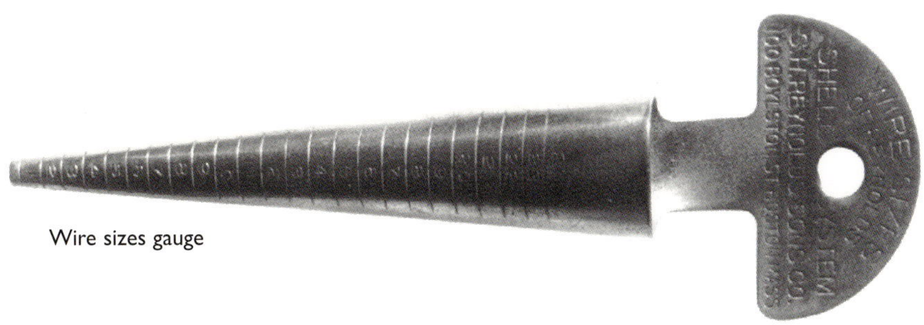

Wire sizes gauge

Folding sheet metal gauge with centimeter scale

What in the world...?

These mysterious objects inhabit a design vacuum.
They are entirely free of artistic pretensions, and their utility and function are more important than their aesthetic value.

However, they are no mystery to the people that use them.

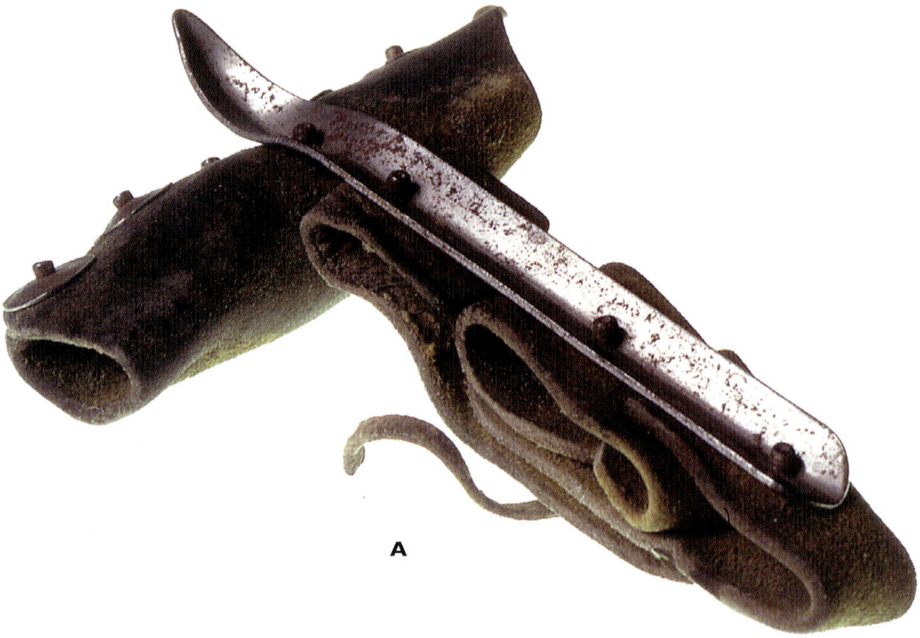

A

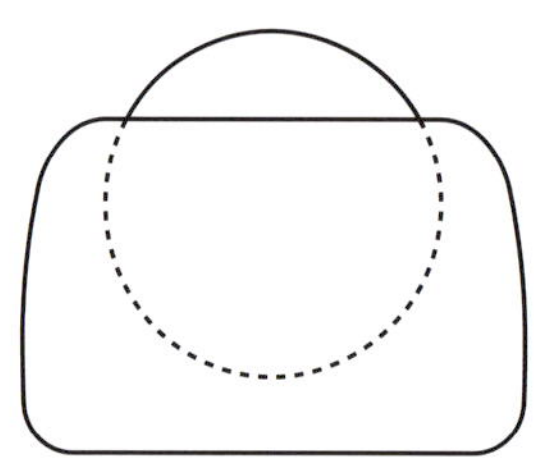

B

C

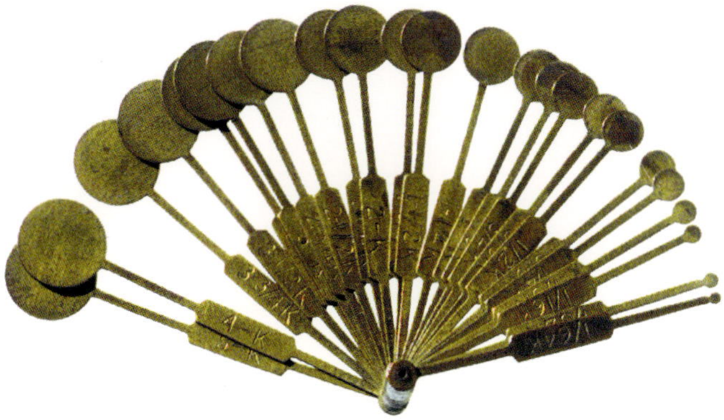

D

A - A corn-sheller for stripping the kernels from the cob.

B - A darning egg with a difference. The loose ball swivels to the areas of the sock that need mending.

The mystery is how the wooden ball got into the smaller opening of the cavity (see drawing).

C - A template used in the British army, to protect the cloth uniform while buttons and other metal adornments are being polished.

D - A diamond "guesstimator" for a fast first assessment of the size of a diamond.

E - An adjustable device to determine the size of the HAT not the HEAD.

E

The path to mechanization

In the middle of the 18th century, mass production began in England with weaving. In America, it began in the 19th century with farming.

With the advent of the assembly line, full mechanization was achieved by 1915. The romance of this period was celebrated by Charlie Chaplin in film, Fernand Léger in painting, and Edgar Varèse in music.

The economics of minimalism is also a common denominator of the three objects illustrated here as they span the three centuries of the Industrial Age.

The crudely forged *window grill*, is cut by hand out of one piece of iron. Proletarian in its raw and awkward energy, it served its purpose of securing homes from malevolent intruders.

Well on its way to mass production, the *corn dryer* is stamped out of a sheet of metal in one piece. Each bent-out arm spears one cob. Every unit is 19″ long and can be combined into multiples by means of male and female connectors. Such 19th century creative thinking gave impetus to 20th century modular design.

The modest *kitchen grater* is an example of the austere beauty of early technology. A sheet of tin pierced with sharp-edged protrusions is transformed into a tool that can shred or grate foods. While kitchen chores haven't changed, technology keeps evolving. The electronic age is marketing ever newer labor-saving devices "that you simply cannot do without."

Window grill in situ

Window grill
Spanish, 18th century

Corn dryer
American, 19th century

Grater
Canadian, 20th century

Ad hoc is...

a form of improvisation which gets its impetus from a variety of sources.

It can be a short term solution using materials at hand, or it can be dictated by a lack of finances. It can be politically inspired, protesting the pretensions of contemporary society. Finally, it may simply be an impatience with doing things by the book.

...making do with whatever is at hand

...innovative adaptation

fix **...do-it-yourself**

TOOT TOOT who's there?

A peek behind the door

Ultimately, the functional, no-nonsense objects we examined earlier, fall by the wayside when the discussion turns to architecture or architectural details. The anonymous industrial vocabulary yields to status and fashion.

Just as clothing is an indicator of the wearer's personality, these entrances can indicate who or what is behind each door. We get a silent message about money, social status and taste.

Door hardware and color schemes have always been an easy way to personalize the cookie-cutter sameness of the bourgeois tract house.

The counter-culture is a design no-man's land, yet can make its point with ingenuity and charm (see also preceding page).

Even the "no style" lever handle of the corporate world evokes an attitude.

Images speak, whether we listen or not.

Portrait of the author as a mythical beast.

George Tscherny began his professional career as a graphic designer in New York City in 1950.

His posters are represented in the permanent collection of the Museum of Modern Art, New York; the Cooper Hewitt Museum, New York; Library of Congress, Washington, D.C.; and the Kunstgewerbemuseum, Zurich.

A comprehensive selection of Tscherny's work is included in the Graphic Design Archives at Rochester Institute of Technology, the Milton Glaser Design Study Center and Archives at the School of Visual Arts, and the electronic database of the Cooper Union School of Art. Over 100 posters and other examples of his work reside in the archives of the Bibliothèque nationale de France.

Tscherny served two terms as president of the American Institute of Graphic Arts (AIGA) and is a member of Alliance Graphique Internationale (AGI).

In 1988, the American Institute of Graphic Arts awarded George Tscherny their annual medal.

In 1992, the School of Visual Arts invited Tscherny to mount a one-man retrospective of his work in "The Masters Series."

In 1997, George Tscherny was inducted into the New York Art Directors Hall of Fame.

In 2007, Tscherny was given a retrospective of his work in the Galerie Blanche at Le Corbusier's La Cité Radieuse in Briey, France.

Maximum Meaning, Minimum Means, covering Tscherny's oeuvre, was published in 2004 by Southeast University Press, China.

George Tscherny is the author of *Changing Faces* published by Princeton Architectural Press in 2005.

Nadia Tscherny is an art historian with an interest in the history of design. She has a Ph.D. in art history from the Institute of Fine Arts, New York University and has published extensively on 18th, 19th and 20th century art. Her articles have appeared in *Art in America*, *The Burlington Magazine*, and *The Magazine Antiques*. She has taught for many years, most recently at New York University and has worked as a curator for The Frick Collection and the Yale Center for British Art, among other institutions.